THE EMERALD CONSPIRACY

Mark Fowler

Designed and illustrated by
Mark Burgess

Series edit

e

s

chael Robinson

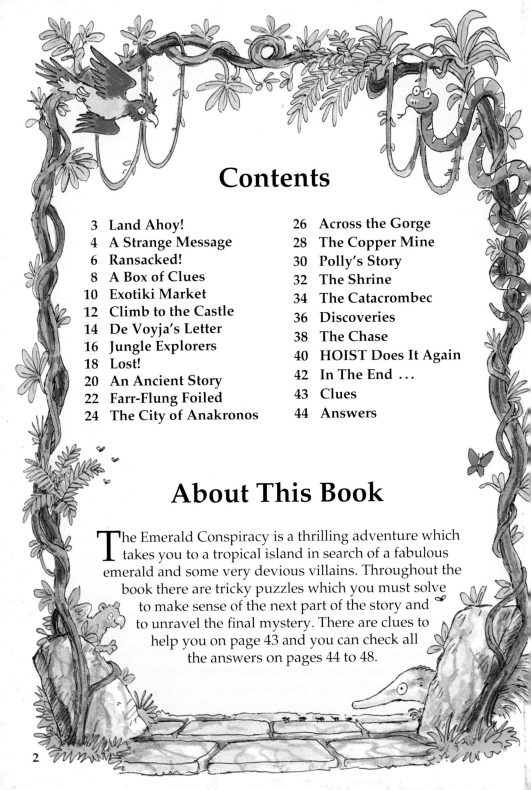

Contents

About This Book

The Emerald Conspiracy is a thrilling adventure which takes you to a tropical island in search of a fabulous emerald and some very devious villains. Throughout the book there are tricky puzzles which you must solve to make sense of the next part of the story and to unravel the final mystery. There are clues to help you on page 43 and you can check all the answers on pages 44 to 48.

Land Ahoy!

As dawn broke over the Exotikan sea, Annie and Joe climbed onto the top deck of the ocean steamer. It was their fifth day at sea and their long journey was nearly at an end. In the distance they could just make out the hazy outline of land. This was their final destination, the tropical island of Exotiki.

"We're nearly there," cried Annie, willing the old steamer to move a little faster.

A whole month on the island lay ahead and the two friends could hardly contain their excitement. Joe pulled out the letter from his cousin Polly and read it for the hundredth time.

Joe

Annie

July 15th

Room 13
The Cockatoo Hotel,
Exotiki Town,
Exotiki.

Dear Annie and Joe,
What great news - you're coming to stay! It's a long journey, but it's all arranged - plane to Ugli City, train to Grime Port, then the slow steamer to Exotiki.
I'm living at an old hotel called the Cockatoo. Once it was the home of Samual De Voyja, the famous pirate and explorer. Now it belongs to my aunt, and it's full of junk and rather run down. In the attic I found an ancient journal. It was written by De Voyja himself in a strange code which I think I've cracked at last.
Can't wait to see you - there's heaps to see and do on this amazing island. I'll meet you at the dock when your boat arrives.
Lots of love,
Polly

P.S. What do you think of these nonsense rhymes from ancient Exotiki? De Voyja's journal is full of them.

There once was a blue Cockatoo
Who slept for a moment or two.
Alas while he napped
The hammock-string snapped
And he fell on a startled gnu.

Then a billy-goat kid said to him:
"I find this exceedingly dim;
Though the lake is as dry
As a rainbow up high
I've been waiting to go for a swim!"

Ancient Exotikan symbols translated by De Voyja

A Strange Message

Several hours later, Annie and Joe stumbled down the gangway onto a bustling quayside. All around them tourists struggled with piles of luggage while parrots and macaws squawked overhead and a strange scent, a mixture of tropical fruit and rotten fish, wafted in the warm sea breeze.

But where was Polly? Joe dumped his battered suitcase on the ground and scanned the faces in the crowd.

As the people slowly drifted away, the two friends found themselves alone. Soon the boat was just a speck on the horizon, but still there was no sign of Polly.

All of a sudden a mountain bike came streaking along the coast road. It hurtled past Annie and Joe, sending them flying into a tropical thornbush.

As they staggered to their feet, they saw an envelope lying on the ground.

"It's addressed to us!" gasped Annie in amazement.

Dear Annie and Joe,
A million apologies! Can't possibly come to the docks. By the time you read this, I'll be somewhere in the Exotikan jungle! Won't be back for weeks, perhaps months. Have a wonderful time on your own.
Lots of love,
Polly.

Quickly, she tore it open. Inside was a letter from Polly, but Annie couldn't believe what it said.

"Polly's left us to fend for ourselves," she exclaimed.

Then Joe noticed something odd about the writing. Behind the cheerful lines, he soon began to uncover a hidden message.

What does the message say?

Ransacked!

Kidnapped? The Cockatoo? What did Polly's hidden message mean?

"The Cockatoo is the name of Polly's hotel," said Joe. "Let's go there straightaway."

But where was it? Annie and Joe set off for the town, but soon they were lost in a maze of backstreets. They stumbled on a bustling market where they stopped to ask for directions, but no one had even heard of the Cockatoo. They hurried on, feeling more and more confused. Then, just as they were giving up hope, they rounded a corner and there it was.

Hesitantly they stepped inside through a crumbling doorway. Now they had to find the rainbow - whatever that might be. There was no one around except for a man snoring loudly at the desk. He was no help at all so they set off in search of Polly's room.

As they opened the door, they stopped and stared in disbelief. Something was very wrong.

"Even Polly's room is never this messy," exclaimed Joe. "It must have been ransacked!"

This confirmed their worst fears. Polly was in dire trouble and they had to help her. Joe gazed around the room and suddenly he saw what they were searching for.

Can you spot it?

A Box of Clues

Joe picked up a small, black box with a rainbow painted on the lid. Crammed inside were bits of paper, including a page from Polly's diary. Perhaps this would help to explain what was going on.

"Polly went to meet someone last night," said Annie, pointing at the last entry on the page. "If we could find out where she went, maybe we could retrace her steps and do some investigating."

The friends pored over the other bits of paper in search of clues, but there was no sign of the one thing that would really help them, a tourist brochure. Could they discover Polly's destination without it?

Where did Polly go last night?

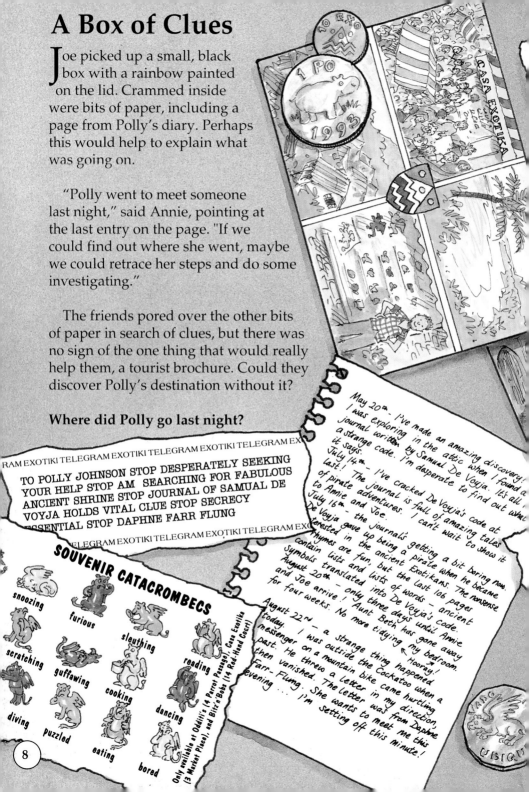

RAM EXOTIKI TELEGRAM EXOTIKI TELEGRAM EXOTIKI TELEGRAM EX

TO POLLY JOHNSON STOP DESPERATELY SEEKING YOUR HELP STOP AM SEARCHING FOR FABULOUS ANCIENT SHRINE STOP JOURNAL OF SAMUAL DE VOYJA HOLDS VITAL CLUE STOP SECRECY ESSENTIAL STOP DAPHNE FARR FLUNG

TELEGRAM EXOTIKI TELEGRAM EXOTIKI TELEGRAM EXO

SOUVENIR CATACROMBECS

snoozing

furious

sleuthing

scratching

guffawing

cooking

reading

diving

puzzled

dancing

eating

bored

Only available at Oddliti's (4 Parrot Passage) Casa Exotika (3 Market Place), and Bitz'n'Bobs (14 Red-Hand Court)

May 20th - I've made an amazing discovery! I was exploring in the attic when I found a journal written by Samual De Voyja. It's all in a strange code. I'm desperate to find out what it says.

July 14th - I've cracked De Voyja's code at last! The journal is full of amazing tales of pirate adventures. I can't wait to show it to Annie and Joe.

July 16th - the journal's getting a bit boring now. De Voyja gave up being a pirate when he became interested in the ancient Exotikans. The nonsense rhymes are fun, but the last 106 pages contain lists and lists of words - ancient symbols translated into De Voyja's code.

August 20th - only three days until Annie and Joe arrive! Aunt Beth has gone away for four weeks. No more tidying my bedroom. Hooray!

August 22nd - a strange thing happened today. I was outside the Cockatoo when a messenger on a mountain bike came hurtling past. He threw a letter in my direction, then vanished. The letter was from Daphne Farr-Flung. She wants to meet me this evening ... I'm setting off this minute!

[Top left newspaper fragment]

arasols," says Exotikan guide Shona Round...
he one place in Exotiki Town that every tourist had to visit...
he bulldozers moved in and this magnificent collonade was razed to the ground. But this is not the only famous Exotiki building to disappear. The Malinga Inn - once the haunt of buccaneers and pirates - has now been demolished, along with all the other buildings in Red-Hand Court.

FARR-FLUNG SEEKS ANCIENT SHRINE

World-famous explorer Daphne Farr-Flung has revealed that she is searching for a fabulous ancient shrine - here on Exotiki! Farr-Flung is hoping to find the long-lost Shrine of the Catacrombec, said to be the most magnificent building ever constructed by the ancient Exotikans. According to legend, the shrine contains a statue of the Catacrombec adorned with a magnificent and priceless emerald.

Daphne Farr-Flung- always to be seen wearing a straw hat and green breeches, and carrying an enormous, bulky backpack.

[Top right]

...LAR SELECTION OF EXOTIKAN SOUVENIRS

STOP PRESS

The SKOOP brings you SENSATIONAL news of a rival bid to find the Shrine of the Catacrombec. Archaeologist Dr. Donald Diggitup, excavating at the ancient city of Anakronos, has unearthed inscriptions which he claims will lead to the shrine.

What's more Diggitup says that he started on his quest months before Daphne Farr-Flung had even heard of the shrine, and he accuses Farr-Flung of being "an imposter and a ransacker of ancient ...tes".

su ins fas Farr stran Catac Parake dense ju accusati Diggitup unearthed fascinating exciting ins Where wi vicious accus lead? Read tomorrow's SKOOP for the latest revelations

For the last word in comfort
THE COCKATOO HOTEL
1, Parrot Passage

DID YOU KNOW?

The Catacrombec is the symbol of modern Exotiki, but two thousand years ago this strange, mythical creature was worshipped as a god. Every year, the ancient Exotikan celebrated the...

THE CASTLE OF PARAKEETS

DIGGITUP - RIVAL QUEST

XANTHE SCURRILUS JAILED FOR ... YEARS.

[Letter]

Room 313
The Cacambo Hotel
August 22nd

Polly,
...ease meet me at eight ...k this evening. It's urgent, ...d secrecy is essential. Come ...o the souvenir shop marked on the enclosed tourist brochure. It's only twenty minutes' walk from the Cockatoo. The door will be open. I'll meet you in the storeroom packed with souvenir Catacrombecs. You MUST bring the journal of Samual De Voyja with you. Tell no one where you are going!

Daphne Farr-Flung

...the mountain bike messenger dropped this by mistake. I wonder what it all means?!

[Code list]

red cooking = successful
yellow snoozing = kidnap
orange snoozing = under
yellow scratching = this
blue dancing = raid
purple guffawing = parakeets
white bored = I
blue diving = to
orange puzzled = mongoose
green cooking = the
yellow sleuthing = base
red reading = prisoner
green reading = timed
purple scratching = at
green diving = returning
orange eating = guard
green guffawing = keep
green snoozing = Saturday
purple dancing = escape
blue eating = helicopter
red furious = by
blue furious = of
green puzzled = am
red puzzled = castle
yellow dancing = for
green furious = is
yellow bored = noon

[De Voyja's Journal]

De Voyja's Journal - Page 89 (DECODED!)
Another ancient nonsense rhyme

One, two, three.
Some hippos went to sea.
Four, five, six,
With the Catacrombec chicks,
Seven, eight, nine.
The sun began to shine.
Ten, eleven, twelve and more,
Then the wind began to roar.

Page 90 (This is just a list of ancient Exotikan symbols)

appears
in/into   emerald
drops   steal
from   priest
thieves   boat
           shrine
           storm
           volcano
           lifts
           escape

9

Exotiki Market

Annie stuffed the papers back into the box and thrust it into her pocket. Pausing only to buy a guidebook, the two friends made their way back to the market place where they had stopped to ask for directions.

They joined the crowds milling around the busy stalls. Then just as a carnival procession passed by, Annie spotted the souvenir shop, locked up and deserted.

This was hopeless. There was nothing to help them find Polly here. Joe gazed gloomily at the dancing pirates and happy faces around him, when all of a sudden something made him look up. Across the square on a balcony, a man with spiky hair was staring at the shop through binoculars.

What was he looking at? Annie and Joe peered through the dusty window at some familiar-looking models. Remembering a scrap of paper from Polly's box, they realized that they were staring at a cryptic message.

What does the message say?

CASA EXOTIKA

HEAD COOK

I ♥ EXOTIKA

11

Climb to the Castle

What did the cryptic message mean? They couldn't be certain, but it looked as if whoever had kidnapped Polly was planning some sort of raid on the Castle of Parakeets. But what could Annie and Joe do now? Should they go to the police and tell them everything?

"There isn't time," said Annie. "We've got to find out about this raid. It might lead us to Polly."

Soon they were climbing the steep path to the Castle of Parakeets, which stood on a cliff top overlooking the sea. But half an hour and 4,476 stone steps later, the castle seemed as far away as ever. The sun beat down fiercely, the steps grew steeper and steeper...

At last, red in the face and gasping, they staggered up the final few steps. It was almost noon. As they reached the outer wall, Joe pulled out the guidebook and began to read. *"Many tourists are put off by the exhausting climb. The Parakeets has few visitors..."* He broke off as Annie let out an indignant cry.

"There's a road," she spluttered, gazing at the hordes of tourists flooding through the gates. "We could have taken the bus!"

They hobbled into a crowded courtyard and collapsed beneath a pillar. All Annie could think about was finding a drink, but she couldn't help overhearing two strangely dressed men talking in loud whispers. They sounded most mysterious.

Annie looked idly at the faces in the crowd. Then, to her surprise, she realized she knew who it was the two men were talking about. What was more, she knew that person's name.

Who are they talking about?

De Voyja's Letter

Who were these men? Why did they suspect Daphne Farr-Flung? Before Annie could think, she saw Joe slinking through a doorway.

"This is the way to the dungeons," he hissed as Annie caught up with him. "If anything fishy is going on, I bet that's where we'll find it!"

Annie began to tell Joe about the two men and their strange conversation, when an ear-splitting scream suddenly shattered the silence.

Robbers! Thieves! Villains and Vagabonds! The Donjon Stones have been stolen.

A lady with a feather duster came tearing around the corner, waving her arms and shouting at the top of her voice. She crashed straight into Annie and Joe, sending them flying.

"What's going on?" asked Annie.

The woman didn't stop to explain. She tore off down the corridor, leaving Annie and Joe staring at a half-open door.

EMERALD
...e shrine.

...some carved stones were ... ...which lead to
...e secret of the ancient symbols, but before I could
...o this donjon. I have written an explanation of the
...e I didde hide before my capture. As for the stones,
...t I ... ...ertain I shall never clappe eyes on...

Samuel De Voyja

...size of an ...
...years ago I did fin...
...shrine. I didde fathom the
...fulfil my quest, I was thrown in...
symbols in my coded Journal, which
I will keep them with me until I die...
the shrine.

The last words of Samuel De Voyja, written...

I have been locked in this donjon a...
life as a pirate and buccaneer. Now...
these are the last words I shalle eve...
Alas, I shall never achieve my fin...
finde the Shrine of the Catacombe...
of all building of ancient Exotik...
the ...
the ...

...the thing of the god unold. It
...repeat, the most Beautious and resplendent
...I quest, for many years I have laboured to
...tonic.
...I am ravaged with feuer and I fear that
...for five long years, praying this pyre for my

6 May 1721

...in the donjon of the Isle of Gonales...

THE DONJON STONES
These ancient carved stones were found in the
dungeon together with this letter. The symbols
carved on the stones have not been deciphered.

They stepped through the doorway into a vast room filled with antiques, and a smashed display case. On the floor they spotted a piece of card and some scraps of old paper.

"These must have come from the case," muttered Annie, trying to read the spidery writing.

Can you fit the pieces of paper together to read the writing?

15

Jungle Explorers

A nnie and Joe slipped out of the room talking in excited whispers.

"De Voyja's letter says that the Donjon Stones lead to the Shrine of the Catacrombec," Annie began. "That must be why they've been stolen."

"But first the thieves would need to decipher the carved symbols," said Joe. "And the key to that is in De Voyja's journal."

"Which Polly found," added Annie. "So that's why she's been kidnapped!"

I heard her say that she's heading for the ancient city of Anakronos . . . in the middle of the jungle.

Just then, they heard the buzzing of rotor blades. Annie remembered the last words of the cryptic message . . ."Escape by helicopter". They raced outside just as a familiar figure climbed aboard. It was Daphne Farr-Flung!

Then you'll need a mega-zoom telescope, vine-cutters and an Explorers' Manual.

Now everything was falling into place. It was Daphne who was interested in De Voyja's journal. It was Daphne who summoned Polly to the souvenir shop. There could be no doubt. Daphne Farr-Flung was Polly's kidnapper.

They had to follow her, but from what they could hear she was heading into the jungle. Undaunted, the friends hurried back into the town and equipped themselves for a jungle expedition. But before setting out, they had to locate Daphne's destination.

Can you find it on the map?

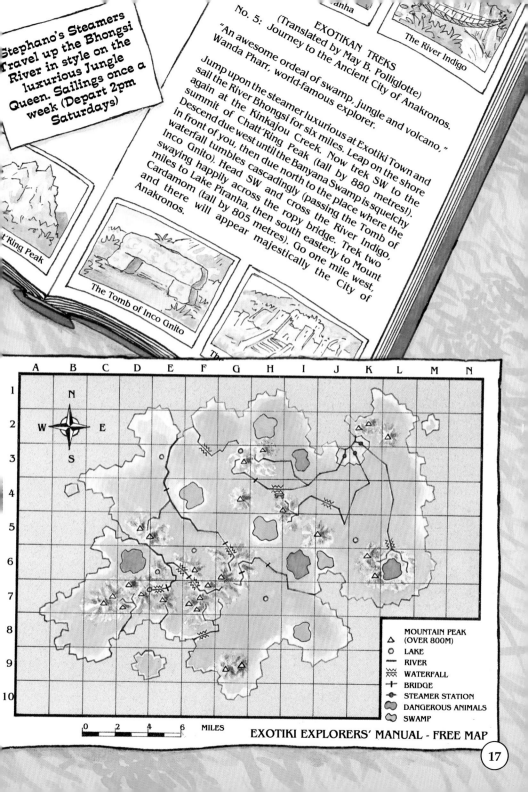

Stephano's Steamers
Travel up the Bhongsi
River in style on the
luxurious Jungle
Queen. Sailings once a
week (Depart 2pm
Saturdays)

The River Indigo

EXOTIKAN TREKS
No. 5: (Translated by May B. Polliglotte)
Journey to the Ancient City of Anakronos.

"An awesome ordeal of swamp, jungle and volcano,"
Wanda Pharr, world-famous explorer.

Jump upon the steamer luxurious at Exotiki Town and
sail the River Bhongsi for six miles. Leap on the shore
again at the Kinkajou Creek. Now trek SW to the
summit of Chatt'Ring Peak (tall by 880 metres!).
Descend due west until the Banyana Swamp is squelchy
in front of you, then due north to the place where the
Inco Gnito). Head SW and cross the River Indigo,
waterfall tumbles cascadingly (passing the Tomb of
swaying happily across the ropy bridge. Trek two
miles to Lake Piranha, then south easterly to Mount
Cardamom (tall by 805 metres). Go one mile west,
and there will appear majestically the City of
Anakronos.

'Ring Peak

The Tomb of Inco Gnito

MOUNTAIN PEAK (OVER 800M)
LAKE
RIVER
WATERFALL
BRIDGE
STEAMER STATION
DANGEROUS ANIMALS
SWAMP

0 2 4 6 MILES

EXOTIKI EXPLORERS' MANUAL - FREE MAP

Lost!

Annie and Joe sprinted to the steamer station, and raced onto the jetty just seconds before the Jungle Queen set sail.

"Jump for it!" screamed Annie, hurling herself up onto the deck. "It's the only boat this week!"

The rusting hulk slowly gathered speed, and soon thick jungle crowded the banks of the River Bhongsi. They forged through alligator-infested waters and past hordes of baboons, as colonies of macaws squawked overhead . . . until at last, after four hot, stifling hours, they reached Kinkajou Creek.

The two friends leaped ashore and watched as the Jungle Queen disappeared into the distance. Then, wielding her vine-cutters, Annie started to hack through the undergrowth. She was still locked in combat with a giant creeper when, just to the left, Joe discovered a ready made path.

"This way!" he cried, setting off deeper into the jungle.

Fearlessly they strode along the path, brushing off swarms of whining mosquitoes. But after three hours, Joe was beginning to suspect they were lost.

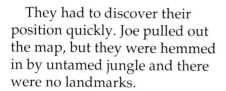

They had to discover their position quickly. Joe pulled out the map, but they were hemmed in by untamed jungle and there were no landmarks.

Then in a flash of inspiration Joe opened the Explorers' Manual. The chapter on rare birds would help.

Where are they?

EXPLORERS' MANUAL - RARE BIRDS OF THE JUNGLE

BIRD	Found in Areas
1. Fan-Tailed Spinning-Bird	D7 N8 J3
2. Pomegranite Bird	B4 F3 J8 L6
3. Shining-Collared Racquet	K3 L6 F8 I6
4. Wing-Snapping Dizzy-Bird	J8 K3 I6 F8
5. Speckled Kazoo	J8 K3 N2 F8
6. Hood-Winked Cacambo	I5 D7 J8 B2
7. Long-Toed Slipper-Bird	I4 D7 L6
8. Crested Blue-wing	N2 F6 I6 J8
9. Violet Sorrow-Bird	H5 I5 L4

An Ancient Story

Joe gulped as he realized that they had strayed into dangerous animal territory. Terrified, the two friends turned and fled.

At last they collapsed in a clearing and checked the map. They were out of danger, but it was getting dark. Night was falling rapidly.

As they climbed into their sleeping bags, a fierce storm broke overhead and the rain trickled into their new extra tough all weather tent.

Dawn broke on a steaming jungle and Annie and Joe woke to find they had pitched their tent right in front of the Tomb of Inco Gnito. They were back on course.

Confidently they plunged back into thick jungle, and by the middle of the morning, they were teetering perilously across the River Indigo.

They strode on as poisonous snakes slithered across their path, and soon they were at the foot of Mount Cardomom.

At midday they reached the summit and excitedly Annie pointed into the distance. They had found the ancient city!

When at last, gasping and exhausted, they reached the ruins of Anakronos, it was like the Castle of Parakeets all over again. The place was already swarming with people. Only this time, they weren't tourists from a bus, but camera crews from helicopters. There was no sign of Daphne Farr-Flung, but Joe recognized someone else.

"It's Dr. Diggitup," he hissed, remembering a newspaper clipping from Polly's box.

Diggitup was talking about some ancient carvings on a broken slab of stone. The pictures and symbols told a strange story.

What is the story?

21

Farr-Flung Foiled

Diggitup's speech was suddenly interrupted by some loud clumping noises, followed by a muffled scream and the unmistakable sounds of a struggle coming from the undergrowth.

A band of uniformed figures burst out of the bushes into the clearing – dragging with them an outraged and spluttering Daphne Farr-Flung!

Instantly, Annie recognized the two men she had overheard at the Castle of Parakeets. The one with the beard pointed an accusing finger at Daphne.

"We are agents from HOIST," he began with a bellow. "Hot Operators Investigating Stolen Treasure. We have reason to believe that you are guilty of stealing the Donjon Stones."

"This is outrageous," Daphne protested. "Let me go this instant."

At that moment Dr. Diggitup strode forward. "What's going on here?" he demanded. "I've known this woman for years. She's no more a thief than I am. Where's your evidence?"

"Right here," said the HOIST agent, flourishing two small scraps of paper.

The City of Anakronos

Annie was about to hurry toward the HOIST agents to tell them about Polly's kidnap, when Joe stopped her. Out of the corner of his eye, he had spotted something very strange.

Someone was creeping stealthily away from the clearing, taking furtive glances behind him. It all seemed highly suspicious.

"It's the man from the market place," exclaimed Joe. "The one with the binoculars."

Perhaps he was an accomplice of Daphne Farr-Flung. If so, he might lead them straight to Polly. Without a second thought, Annie and Joe followed as the man disappeared through a crack in the walls of the ancient city.

They followed him through a series of underground passages and out into an overgrown courtyard that was open to the sky. Annie and Joe hid as the man pulled out a radio transmitter and began to gabble urgently into the microphone. He was sending some kind of message, but it made no sense.

Without thinking, Annie jotted down the jumbled words. For some reason, they seemed familiar.

Then Joe remembered a piece of paper from Polly's box. He knew exactly how to make sense of the message.

Can you decipher the message?

Across the Gorge

There was no doubt in Joe's mind. Polly was the "prisoner" and the "Mongoose" was one of her kidnappers, in league with Daphne Farr-Flung. The two friends followed as the man dived through a concealed doorway into a long, dark tunnel. On and on they raced, through the blackness...

...and burst out into daylight on a ledge high above a gorge. Joe pointed across the torrent, shouting above the crashing and pounding of the water. The man was on the other side. Joe stared at the terrifying maze of bridges. They had to find a way across.

Can you see a safe route?

The Copper Mine

The sun was setting over the jungle when at last Annie and Joe staggered onto safe ground. As they paused for breath on the far side of the gorge, Annie pointed into the valley below.

"Daphne's spiky haired accomplice must have been heading for those buildings," she hissed, already scrambling down the hillside. "Let's go and investigate."

As they crept through a gap in the fence, Joe spotted a sign. They were inside the Doloroso Copper Mine.

Lurking in the shadows and keeping low, Joe opened the guidebook at D for Doloroso... *"This was once the wealthiest mine on the entire island. Now it is abandoned and deserted..."* At that moment Annie heard voices...

No one can tackle the Exotikan jungle at night. We'll set off for the shrine at dawn.

Where's the prisoner?

Suspended half-way down the main mineshaft, inside the cage. Tee hee!

They had to find the main mineshaft. They dodged past heaps of rusting machinery and weaved through the derelict buildings. At last they found themselves staring at a complex system of cogs and pulleys.

"The cage must be attached to the rope going down the mineshaft," said Annie trying to fathom out how it all worked. "We just need to winch it up and hope Polly's inside."

Which handle should they turn?

Polly's Story

With trembling hands, they set the machinery in motion. The gears began to grind and the wheels turned. Annie and Joe craned forward, peering into the darkness. Was Polly really there?

"I knew you'd find me!" hissed an excited voice as the cage neared the surface. It WAS Polly! "When my kidnappers forced me to write that letter, I was sure you'd spot my hidden message," she added as Annie and Joe eagerly helped her out of the cage.

The trio crept out of the mine to safety. Then Polly began to recount her adventures ...

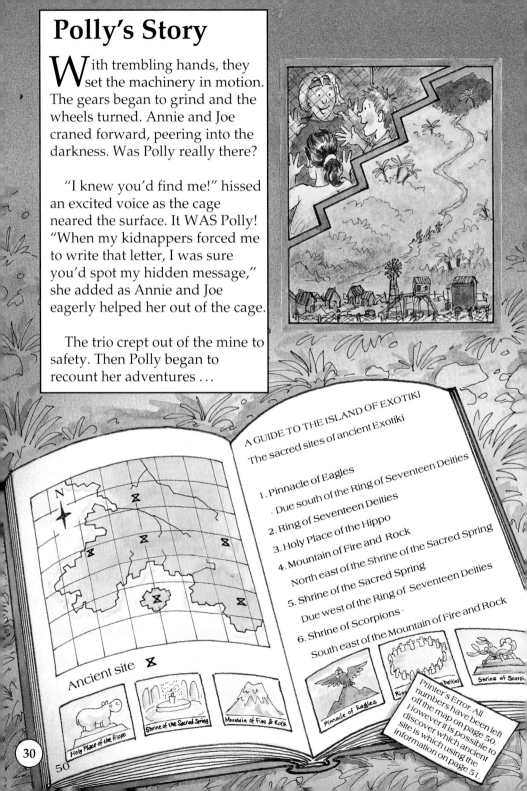

A GUIDE TO THE ISLAND OF EXOTIKI

The sacred sites of ancient Exotiki

1. Pinnacle of Eagles
   Due south of the Ring of Seventeen Deities

2. Ring of Seventeen Deities

3. Holy Place of the Hippo

4. Mountain of Fire and Rock
   North east of the Shrine of the Sacred Spring

5. Shrine of the Sacred Spring
   Due west of the Ring of Seventeen Deities

6. Shrine of Scorpions.
   South east of the Mountain of Fire and Rock

Ancient site ✗

Holy Place of the Hippo

Shrine of the Sacred Spring

Mountain of Fire & Rock

Pinnacle of Eagles

Ring ... Deities

Shrine of Scorpi...

Printer's Error. All numbers have been left off the map on page 50. However it is possible to discover which ancient site is which using the information on page 51.

50

Finding the shrine will be very difficult. The symbols on the stones don't seem to be directions at all. They are all about the flight of a bird, and the route the bird takes is the key to the position of the shrine.

… "I was on my way to the souvenir shop when two masked figures grabbed me and bundled me into an ice cream van. The next thing I knew, I was at the mine. There's a conspiracy. The gang who kidnapped me are planning to steal the emerald from the Shrine of the Catacrombrec. They forced me to use my knowledge of De Voyja's journal to decipher the Donjon Stones, and now they are ready to raid the shrine".

Now Polly was free, the three friends were determined to thwart the thieving villains, and Polly had a plan. She produced a copy of the symbols carved on the stones, complete with translation. With the help of the guidebook they could locate the shrine, and perhaps they could beat the villains to it.

Where is the shrine?

Imagine that a bird flies from the Mountain of Fire and Rock to the Shrine of the Sacred Spring, then to the Ring of Seventeen Deities, then on to the Holy Place of the Hippo, then to the Shrine of Scorpions, and finally to the Pinnacle of Eagles. If the bird flies always in straight lines, then verily it will pass above the Shrine of the Catacrombec twice.

The Shrine

At the first glimmer of dawn Annie, Joe and Polly set off into the jungle, heading south. Struggling through the dense undergrowth, they scrambled over fallen trees and hacked at vines and creepers, until they reached a raging torrent.

"We'll have to wade across!" cried Joe, plunging into the racing waters.

They dragged themselves onto the far bank, but there was no time to rest. They struggled on, bitten by mosquitoes and torn by the undergrowth as the jungle became thicker and thicker. At last they sensed their journey was nearly over. They burst through a wall of giant creepers and stopped dead. Awestruck, they gazed up at a massive stone doorway carved into the cliff face.

"This is it," stammered Polly. "The Shrine of the Catacrombec!"

As they crept closer, a hush seemed to fall over the jungle, and Joe felt an eerie sensation of malevolent eyes watching from the undergrowth. Two gigantic doors towered above them, barring the entrance. How could they get inside? Polly had the answer.

How can they open the doors?

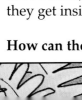

The Catacrombec

The doors slid silently open to reveal a steep staircase. Trembling with excitement, Annie, Joe and Polly tiptoed down the steps and found themselves in a magnificent chamber. In front of them, on a huge stone plinth, reared the image of the Catacrombec. Menacing and majestic, it glared at them proudly. But Joe realized that something was wrong.

"The emerald..." he stammered. "It's not there!"

"And where did these come from?" gasped Polly, snatching up some scraps of paper from the floor.

Had the villains beaten them to it? At that moment the friends heard footsteps...

To Peter da Plunda, 25th August
I have the emerald. Meet me at the Cacambo Hotel at 10am tomorrow to arrange the hand-over. If you try any tricks, I will hurl you into a Banyana swamp.
Daphne Farr-Flung

23rd August
To Daphne Farr-Flung,
I met Xanthe Sunrilus at the Malinga Inn today. Everything is arranged for the kidnap this evening.
Peter da Plunda.

This is an incredible moment – we are undoubtedly the first people to set foot inside the shrine for two thousand years.

"Hide!" hissed Annie, diving for cover.

As the footsteps came closer, the friends crouched behind a pillar. They looked at the pieces of paper Polly had found.

"They must have been dropped by the thieves," said Joe. But there were several things about the two messages which did not make sense.

What are they?

Discoveries

Annie and Joe were still staring at the scraps of paper when, to their amazement, Dr. Diggitup strode into the chamber, surrounded by a film crew.

Ahhh! The emerald has been STOLEN! But look, the thieves have left evidence - down there...

As the archaeologist looked up at the Catacrombec, he let out a dramatic howl of rage. Then he began to race around the shrine as if searching for something. Whatever it was, he couldn't find it. He grew more and more frantic, darting this way and that, his eyes pinned to the floor until, all of a sudden, Daphne Farr-Flung appeared!

or there...

or somewhere...

Daphne had escaped from the HOIST agents, but had she stolen the emerald? Diggitup had no doubts. He pointed an accusing finger at the explorer...

but wait... no evidence is needed...

That woman is the thief!

At that moment, another bunch of visitors bounded into the shrine. It was the HOIST agents again, in hot pursuit of Daphne Farr-Flung.

"You thought you'd got away," bellowed the man with the beard, hurling himself across the chamber at Daphne. "But we followed you to this heathen temple, and this time there'll be no escape."

Meanwhile, one of the reporters was valiantly trying to make sense of events. Ignoring the chaos, he began to explain how Diggitup had found his way to the shrine.

Annie watched as the man held up a piece of paper to the camera. It was then that she realized something was very wrong.

What has Annie realized?

The Chase

Diggitup's inscriptions were nothing but nonsense. They could never have led to the shrine, so how had he found it?

"He must have seen the Donjon Stones," said Polly. "What's more, he must have seen my translation of the symbols, which can mean only one thing. He's one of the villains!"

In a flash, Annie rushed forward, accusing Diggitup. But the archaeologist flung himself across the shrine to a hidden tunnel. Annie, Joe and Polly leaped after him, closely followed by everyone else. They stampeded along the passage and burst out above a gorge, just as Diggitup launched himself into mid air ...

Annie, Joe and all the others set off in hot pursuit. They crossed the gorge and ran for what felt like miles down a steep hillside. Faster and faster they went, until at last they skidded to a halt on top of a cliff … just as Diggitup vanished over the edge on the end of a rope.

The HOIST agents made a desperate bid to follow him, but already the archaeologist was aboard a motor boat, and he wasn't alone.

"They're getting away," cried Joe. But the HOIST agents weren't beaten yet.

Bring in the HOISTcopter

HOIST Does It Again

At that moment, a flash of lightning streaked across the darkening sky. There was a crash of thunder and hurricane force winds hit the island. As masssive waves pounded against the cliff, Joe pointed to the villains' boat.

"They're heading straight for a whirlpool!" he screamed.

The boat edged closer and closer to the vortex. Then out of the raging tempest, a HOIST helicopter appeared, battling against the violent winds. With lightning speed, the HOIST agents winched the villains off the deck, just seconds before the boat was swallowed up by the power of the swirling water.

It's just like the story told by the carvings at Anakronos - a giant bird swoops from the sky and plucks the villains from the stormy seas. This is Orlando O'Nair, live from the Exotiki jungle.

Minutes later, Diggitup and the other villains from the boat were led off the helicopter, handcuffed to HOIST agents. Annie recognized the spiky haired man. He didn't look much like a crook, but then neither did Diggitup.

"Another mystery solved," boasted one of the HOIST agents, as he inspected his captives.

Annie and Joe were still feeling confused when Polly dashed up to them, clutching a notebook … and the EMERALD!

"Diggitup dropped these as he tried to escape," she said.

Astounded, the friends gazed at the magnificent jewel. Then they opened the book. Perhaps this would explain what had been going on.

What does it say?

In The End...

Diggitup's conspiracy was thwarted and at last the mystery was solved. Soon the scheming archaeologist and his cronies were behind bars, Daphne Farr-Flung was free again and Annie, Joe and Polly were able to begin their holiday. And with her aunt still away, Polly was in no hurry to tidy her bedroom!

Dear Polly, Joe and Annie,

How can I ever thank you enough? If it hadn't been for you, Dr Dastardly Diggitup's conspiracy would have succeeded - and I would be rotting in jail at this very moment!

It all began five years ago when I was exploring around Lake Konundrum. I discovered that Diggitup was planning to plunder the tomb of King Enigmatik IV. I come across him again in the Thundercrash Mountains where he was stealing ceremonial masks worth millions. Soon I had evidence that he had plundered hundreds of ancient sites. I was about to expose him when he put Operation Catacrombec into action. Thanks to you, the whole conspiracy back-fired!

If you are ever in the mood for adventure, why don't you join me on one of my expeditions? I can always be contacted at The Jolly Adventurers Inn.

Enjoy the rest of your stay on Exotiki!

Daphne Farr-Flung

Diggitup - slammed up!

Within hours of his arrest, undercover investigators swooped on Diggitup's million-dollar mansion. Hidden in a specially built vault, they found priceless treasures - and enough evidence to put the double-crossing archaeologist away for a long, long time.

Stolen treasures

Diggitup's fellow conspirators were named as Ricardo Bizarro, owner of the Casa Exotika souvenir shop; Signora Doloroso, a member of the old Exotikan mining family; and Harry Hoakes, a well-known fraudster.

As the conniving conspirators were taken away by helicopter, the three plucky kids who had unravelled the mystery returned the stolen emerald to the shrine. Watched by HOIST agent Mac "the Beard" Bellows, they lifted the jewel back into its rightful place with trembling hands. At once the storm died away. Sunlight streamed into the chamber of the Catacrombec, filling it with an unearthly green light.

Clues

Answers

Pages 4-5

The strange-looking letters in Polly's note are actually ancient Exotikan symbols. If you use De Voyja's translations of the ancient Exotikan nonsense rhymes (page 3) you will find that the symbols spell out this message:

I've been kidnapped. Go to the Cockatoo and find the rainbow.

Pages 6-7

The rainbow is here.

Pages 8-9

In her letter, Daphne asks to meet Polly in a shop which stocks Souvenir Catacrombecs. According to a document in Polly's box, these are sold in only three places: Odditi's (4 Parrot Passage), Casa Exotika (3 Market Place) and Bitz'n'Bobs (14 Red-Hand Court).

But which did Polly go to?

The article above the photograph of Daphne Farr-Flung states that all the buildings in Red-Hand Court have been demolished, so Bitz'n'Bobs can no longer exist. Odditi's is in Parrot Passage, and we know from the advertisement under Daphne's photograph that the Cockatoo is in the same street. The correct shop is twenty minutes walk from the Cockatoo, and so cannot be Odditi's. Polly must therefore have gone to Casa Exotika.

Pages 10-11

The models in the window are Souvenir Catacrombecs. The scrap of paper dropped by the mountain bike messenger (in Polly's rainbow box on page 9) is the key to a secret code. Each model has a hidden meaning, depending on its colour and what it is doing.

The decoded message is:

Kidnap successful. Raid at Castle of Parakeets timed for noon Saturday. Escape by helicopter.

Pages 12-13

The uniformed men are talking about Daphne Farr-Flung. Annie recognizes her from the description and photograph in the newspaper clipping on page 9.

Pages 14-15

The pieces of paper can be fitted together to make the following letter:

The last words of Samuel De Voyja, written in the donjon of the Castle of Porokets

6th May 1721

I have been locked in this donjon for five long years, paying the price for my life as a pirate and buccaneer. Now I am ravaged with fever and I fear that these are the last words I shalle ever write.

Alas, I shall never achieve my final quest. For many years I have laboured to finde the Shrine of the Catacumbee, by repute the most beauteous and resplendent of all buildings of ancient Exotiki. Legend doth tell that a wondrous EMERALD the size of an ox's hoof doth adorn the image of the god inside the shrine.

Six years ago I did find some carved stones with inscriptions which lead to the shrine. I didde fathom the secret of the ancient symbols, but before I could fulfil my quest, I was thrown into this donjon. I have written an explanation of the symbols in my coded journal, whiche I didde hide before my capture. As for the stones, I will keep them with me until I die, but I am certain I shall never clappe eyes on the shrine.

Samuel De Voyja

Pages 16-17

There are three steamer stations which could be the start of the route. Two routes fail after a few miles, but only the correct one passes the Tomb of Inco Gnito. The route is marked in red. The Ancient City is at the bottom of square F6.

Tomb of Inco Gnito

The Ancient City of Anakronos

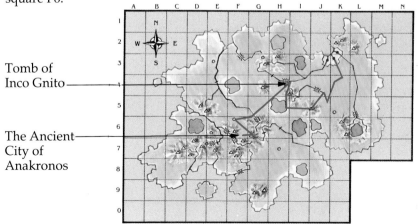

Pages 18-19

Many of the birds look very similar to those shown in the Explorers'
Manual, but are not quite the same. The rare birds that Annie and Joe
match exactly with those in the book are the Shining-Collared Racquet, the
Wing-Snapping Dizzy-Bird and the Crested Blue-Wing. The information in
the Manual shows that these birds are only found together in square I6.
Annie and Joe realize from the map on page 17 that this area is inhabited
by dangerous animals.

Pages 20-21

Whatever Diggitup says, it is fairly easy to piece together the broken slabs
of the frieze to reconstruct the panel. The story told by the beautiful
carvings can be deciphered by using the key to the symbols on page 9. The
symbols translate as follows:

Thieves steal emerald from Catacrombec shrine. Escape in boat. Storm.
Catacrombec appears. Lifts thieves. Drops in volcano.

This is what the stones look like when pieced together.

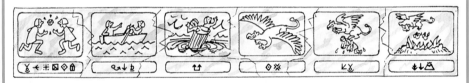

Pages 22-23

The coded message reads in the
usual way, from left to right and
from top to bottom. But every other
letter is upside down and back to
front. When all the letters are
written correctly, this is what the
message says:

To Peter Da Plunda
Everything is arranged for the raid
at the Castle of Parakeets. We will
strike at noon on Saturday.
Daphne Farr-Flung

Pages 24-25

This is another version of the
Souvenir Catacrombec code.
To crack it, once again use the
scrap of paper dropped by the
mountain bike messenger in
Polly's box on page 9.

When deciphered the message
reads:

This is the Mongoose.
I am returning to base.
Keep the prisoner under guard.

Pages 26-27

The safe route is shown here in black.

Pages 28-29

The middle handle must be turned this way ↻. This will lower the basket of rocks to raise the cage without setting off the alarm bells. The red arrows show the way that each part of the mechanism works.

Pages 30-31

The ancient sites should be labelled as shown here. The bird's path of flight is marked in black.

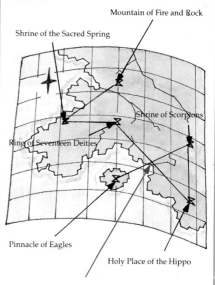

Mountain of Fire and Rock

Shrine of the Sacred Spring

Shrine of Scorpions

Ring of Seventeen Deities

Pinnacle of Eagles

Holy Place of the Hippo

The shrine is here. It is the only place the bird passes over twice.

Pages 32-33

All the Exotikan number symbols are shown in the nonsense rhyme on page 9. The numbers on the doorlock are therefore:

32	20	72	24
5	7	16	36
8	6	10	9
14	64	12	4

The sequence of buttons which will open the door is:

4, 8, 16, 32, 64

Pages 36-37

These inscriptions can be found on page 3. They are nothing but an ancient nonsense rhyme and could not possibly have led Diggitup to the shrine.

Pages 34-35

The first letter, dated August 25th, implies that Daphne is still at large. As far as we know, she has been a prisoner of the HOIST agents since the 24th. . .

Several things are suspicious about the second letter. We know from the documents on page 9 that Polly was kidnapped on August 22nd, but here the date is the 23rd. It is unlikely that Xanthe Scurrilus would be meeting anyone – a newspaper headline on page 9 says that she has been jailed. It is even more unlikely that a meeting was held at the Malinga Inn, as another article on page 9 states that this has been demolished.

Pages 40-41

In order to read Diggitup's diary, first turn the book upside down, then correct every other letter by turning it back to front and upside down. You will need to add the punctuation. This is what the diary says:

Operation Catacrombec

August 1st. At last I can rid myself of that meddling explorer. This is my plan. With the help of my three loyal cronies, I will kidnap Polly Johnson, then steal the Donjon Stones and raid the Shrine of the Catacrombec. Meanwhile, I will send fake evidence to HOIST. They will start to investigate, and soon they will be sure that Daphne Farr-Flung is behind all these crimes. Finally, I will plant the emerald itself in her room at the Cacambo Hotel. I will lose a priceless jewel, but Farr-Flung will be thrown in jail, never to trouble me again!
August 2nd. This is my chance to get my revenge on that double-crossing scoundrel, Peter Da Plunda, who nearly ruined Operation Konundrum. I will make the HOIST agents believe that he is Farr-Flung's accomplice, then he too will be clapped in irons.
August 24th. The HOIST agents have struck too early. How can Farr-Flung raid the shrine if she is already a prisoner? I will disguise myself and release her.

Isn't it a coincidence that this is in the same code as "Daphne's" message on page 23? Perhaps Diggitup wrote that too!

This edition first published in 2007 by Usborne Publishing Ltd.,
Usborne House, 83-85 Saffron Hill, London EC1N 8RT, England.
www.usborne.com Copyright © 2007, 2002, 1993 Usborne Publishing Ltd.
Illustrations copyright © 2007, 2002, 1993 Mark Burgess (except cover illustrations)

All rights reserved. No part of this publication may be reproduced, stored in a retrieval system or transmitted in any form or by any means, electronic, mechanical, photocopying, recording or otherwise without the prior permission of the publisher. The name Usborne and the devices ♀☺ are Trade Marks of Usborne Publishing Ltd. Printed in China.